Dear Parent:
Your child's love of reading starts here!

Every child learns to read in a different way and at his or her own speed. Some go back and forth between reading levels and read favorite books again and again. Others read through each level in order. You can help your young reader improve and become more confident by encouraging his or her own interests and abilities. From books your child reads with you to the first books he or she reads alone, there are I Can Read Books for every stage of reading:

SHARED READING
Basic language, word repetition, and whimsical illustrations, ideal for sharing with your emergent reader

BEGINNING READING
Short sentences, familiar words, and simple concepts for children eager to read on their own

READING WITH HELP
Engaging stories, longer sentences, and language play for developing readers

READING ALONE
Complex plots, challenging vocabulary, and high-interest topics for the independent reader

ADVANCED READING
Short paragraphs, chapters, and exciting themes for the perfect bridge to chapter books

I Can Read Books have introduced children to the joy of reading since 1957. Featuring award-winning authors and illustrators and a fabulous cast of beloved characters, I Can Read Books set the standard for beginning readers.

A lifetime of discovery begins with the magical words "I Can Read!"

Visit www.icanread.com for information
on enriching your child's reading experience.

Thank You, Amelia Bedelia

Story by Peggy Parish

Pictures by Barbara Siebel Thomas

based on the original drawings by Fritz Siebel

HarperCollinsPublishers

Thank You, Amelia Bedelia Text copyright © 1964 by Margaret Parish Text copyright renewed 1992 by the Estate of Margaret Parish Illustrations copyright © 1964 by Fritz Siebel Illustrations copyright renewed 1992 by the Estate of Fritz Siebel Revised illustrations copyright © 1993 by the Estate of Fritz Siebel All rights reserved. No part of this book may be used or reproduced in any manner whatsoever without written permission except in the case of brief quotations embodied in critical articles and reviews. Manufactured in China. For information address HarperCollins Children's Books, a division of HarperCollins Publishers, 195 Broadway, New York, NY 10007. www.harpercollinschildrens.com

Library of Congress Cataloging-in-Publication Data

Parish, Peggy.
  Thank you, Amelia Bedelia / story by Peggy Parish ; pictures by Barbara Siebel Thomas, based on the original drawings by Fritz Siebel.—Newly illustrated edition
      p.   cm.—(An I can read book)
  Summary: Preparing for the arrival of an important visitor, a wacky housekeeper follows her employer's instructions with humorous results.
    ISBN-10: 0-06-022979-9 (trade bdg.) — ISBN-13: 978-0-06-022979-5 (trade bdg.)
    ISBN-10: 0-06-022980-2 (lib. bdg.) — ISBN-13: 978-0-06-022980-1 (lib. bdg.)
    ISBN-10: 0-06-444171-7 (pbk.) — ISBN-13: 978-0-06-444171-1 (pbk.)
    [1. Household employees—Fiction. 2. Humorous stories.] I. Thomas, Barbara Siebel, ill. II. Title. III. Series.
PZ7.P219 Th 1993   92-5746
[E]—dc20   CIP
                                                                                                                              AC

                                      15 16 SCP 20 19 18 17 16 15 14
                        ❖ Original edition published 1964. Newly illustrated I Can Read edition, 1993.

For Ann, Jack, and Brad Rost

Mrs. Rogers was all in a dither.
"Great-Aunt Myra
is coming today."
"Now, that is nice,"
said Amelia Bedelia.
"I do love company."

"We've been trying for years
to get her to visit,"
said Mrs. Rogers,
"but Great-Aunt Myra says
the only place she feels at home
is at home.
So everything must be exactly right.
We do want her to be happy here."
"Now don't you worry your head,"
said Amelia Bedelia.
"I'll fix everything.
What should I do first?"

"Well, the guest room
must be made ready.
Strip the sheets off the bed.
Remake it
with the new rosebud sheets,"
said Mrs. Rogers.
"Thank goodness you're here."

Amelia Bedelia went

to the guest room.

"These folks do have odd ways.

Imagine stripping sheets

after you use them."

Amelia Bedelia shook her head.

But she stripped those sheets.

Amelia Bedelia had just finished
when the doorbell rang.
"That must be the laundryman
with Mr. Rogers's shirts,"
called Mrs. Rogers.
"Please check them
and make sure
they're all there."
Amelia Bedelia hurried to the door
and took the package.

Amelia Bedelia opened the package.

She unfolded each shirt.

"Two sleeves, one collar,
one pocket, and six buttons.
Yes, they're all here."

"There's not a thing missing,"
said Amelia Bedelia.
"Now to check them.
It would be a sight easier
to buy them already checked,"
said Amelia Bedelia.
But she quickly checked each shirt.

Mrs. Rogers

came downstairs in a rush.

"Amelia Bedelia,

my bright pink dress

has spots in it.

Please remove them

with this spot remover.

Leave the dress out.

I will wear it tonight.

Now I must go to the market."

Amelia Bedelia looked
at the bright pink dress.
"I don't see any spots.
This dress just needs washing."
Then another dress
caught Amelia Bedelia's eye.

"She must have meant
her light pink dress.
Now that one sure is spotted."
Amelia Bedelia held the dress up.
"It looks mighty nice
with the spots in it.
But I guess
she's tired of it that way."

Amelia Bedelia put spot remover
on each spot.
Then she waited.
Nothing happened.

"Didn't think
that stuff would work,"
said Amelia Bedelia.
She got the scissors.
And Amelia Bedelia
removed every spot from that dress.

"Amelia Bedelia,"
called Mrs. Rogers.
"Please take these groceries."
Amelia Bedelia ran
to take the bag.

"Here are some roses, too.

Do scatter them

around the living room.

I must get my hair done now.

While I'm gone,

wash all the vegetables

and string the beans.

If you have time,

make a jelly roll.

Great-Aunt Myra

does love jelly roll,"

said Mrs. Rogers.

Amelia Bedelia stopped
in the living room.
"Seems like roses would look nicer
sitting proper-like in vases.
But if she wants them scattered,
scattered they will be."

Amelia Bedelia went on
to the kitchen with the groceries.
She washed all the vegetables.

Then she found a ball of string.

And Amelia Bedelia

strung all those beans.

33

"Jelly! Roll!"

exclaimed Amelia Bedelia.

"I never heard tell

of jelly rolling."

But Amelia Bedelia

got out a jar of jelly.

Amelia Bedelia tried

again and again.

But she just could not get

that jelly to roll.

Amelia Bedelia washed her hands.

She got out a mixing bowl.

Amelia Bedelia began to mix

a little of this

and a pinch of that.

"Great-Aunt Myra
or no Great-Aunt Myra—
there's not going to be
any rolling jelly
in this house tonight,"
said Amelia Bedelia.

Mr. and Mrs. Rogers arrived home
at the same time.

Mrs. Rogers called,

"Amelia Bedelia,

please separate three eggs

and pare the other vegetables

you washed.

I'll do the cooking."

Then she and Mr. Rogers

hurried upstairs to dress.

Amelia Bedelia took out three eggs.
"I wonder why they need
to be separated.
They've been together all day
and nothing happened."
But Amelia Bedelia
separated those eggs.

"Pair the vegetables!"

Amelia Bedelia laughed.

"Here, you two go together—

and you two.

Now be careful,

or I'll be separating you, too."

Amelia Bedelia

went up to Mrs. Rogers's room.

"What should I do

with these stripped sheets?"

she asked.

"Stripped sheets!"

exclaimed Mrs. Rogers.

But she got no further.

Mr. Rogers roared,

"What in thunderation

happened to my shirts?"

"Oh, don't you like big checks?

I didn't have time

to do little ones.

But I will next time,"

promised Amelia Bedelia.

"My dress!" exclaimed Mrs. Rogers.

"It's full of holes."

"Yes, ma'am, I removed

every single spot,"

said Amelia Bedelia.

Before Mrs. Rogers
could say any more,
the doorbell rang.
"Great-Aunt Myra,"
said Mr. and Mrs. Rogers.
They rushed to the front door.

"Good evening, grandniece.

Good evening, grandnephew.

My, that trip made me hungry,"

said Great-Aunt Myra.

"I'll cook dinner right now,"
said Mrs. Rogers.
Everybody went into the kitchen.

"Amelia Bedelia,
did you string the beans?"
asked Mrs. Rogers.
"Yes. See—they do
give such a homey look,"
said Amelia Bedelia.

"Where are the eggs

I asked you to separate?"

said Mrs. Rogers.

"Here's one,

one is behind the clock,

and the other is over there.

Did I separate them

far enough apart?"

asked Amelia Bedelia.

Mrs. Rogers said nothing.

So Amelia Bedelia went on.

"And I paired the vegetables.
They went together real well,
and there weren't any left over."

Mrs. Rogers slapped her hand

on the table.

It hit right in a sticky blob.

"Ugh! What is that?"

she shouted.

"Jelly. I tried to make it roll.

But it just plip-plopped

all over the place,"

said Amelia Bedelia.

"Amelia Bedelia!"

exclaimed Mrs. Rogers.

"How do you get things so mixed up?"

"Things mixed up!
Oh, I plumb forgot,"
said Amelia Bedelia.
She hurried to the stove.

Amelia Bedelia
opened the oven door.
Great-Aunt Myra sat up straight
and sniffed.

"Hot apple pie! I do declare.
Now that's the kind of
mixed-up thing I like."

Great-Aunt Myra announced,

"Grandniece, grandnephew,

I like it here."

"Oh, Great-Aunt Myra,

we're so glad!"

said Mr. and Mrs. Rogers.

They both began to talk at once.

But Great-Aunt Myra

wasn't much for words.

She had her eyes

on that last piece of pie.

Great-Aunt Myra put

the last piece of pie

on her plate.

Then she said,

"Grandniece, grandnephew,

I will visit you often.

That Amelia Bedelia really knows

how to make a body feel at home.

Thank you, Amelia Bedelia."

Amelia Bedelia smiled.

She and Great-Aunt Myra

would get along.